EIGHT SEVENTEEN

BY

Alan T. Russell

Chapter One – Where It All Began

It was one of those classic English summer days — the kind that made the tarmac bubble like it was trying to escape the road. The heat wrapped around you like clingfilm, and even the shade felt like it was holding its breath.

Darren and I were seventeen, working our way through the summer holidays for his sister's boyfriend, Andy — a car dealer who bought and sold motors from his place near the old Mile Oak pub. We weren't just giving cars a rinse. We were **valeting**. Full interiors, shampoo, polish, the works. Four cars a day, every day.

Andy paid us **£40 per car**.
That's **£160 each, per day** — in the 90s.
It felt like we'd cracked some kind of cheat code. Pints were cheap back then. You could live like a king on that kind of cash.

But Andy had this thing about messing with us.

Now and then, he'd wave our wages in front of us with that grin of his and say:

> "Double or nothing, lads?"

We'd look at each other — sunburnt, knackered, hands raw from scrubbing alloys — and weigh it up. Double was tempting. *Really* tempting. But the thought of walking home with nothing after a full day in that heat? That was a hard pill to swallow.

Sometimes we said yes.
We never lost.

Other times we said no, and Andy would laugh, shake his head like we were old men with no guts, and still pay us anyway.

Looking back, I reckon I was lucky back then.
I mean... *really* lucky.
But sometimes I wonder if it was something else entirely.

Darren and I were both around five-seven — though somehow he always seemed taller. Maybe it was the way he carried himself. He was different. Brilliant, but strange. Genius-level smart. He didn't revise for exams. Didn't need to. His answers came from somewhere no one else could see. Even the teachers couldn't figure out how he worked — but his grades spoke for themselves.

He lived in a mansion in Middleton — four and a half acres of land, a brook running through the back field, and a living room with a fireplace that looked like it had been dragged in from a castle. He fit in there.

And me? I was his scruffy mate from Walmley.
No money. No genius. Just cheek and persistence.

Maybe I wore him down. Or maybe he saw something in me that other people didn't.
Whatever it was, we became inseparable.

We both loved our games. Loved the pub.
Loved trying to chat up girls — even though we'd turn red and trip over our words half the time.

That day, we finished up, pockets full of Andy's cash, and headed toward The Green Man — the pub down the road from Darren's. Pints, chips, maybe a glance across the bar if someone smiled. That was the plan.

Then it'd be back to Darren's, the night still warm, the Amiga loaded up, the two of us shouting across the room while the glow of the screen flickered off the dark.

We didn't know it yet…
But that night — that perfect, nothing-special night — would be the last one we'd ever look back on as normal.

Chapter Two – The Green Man

By the time we got to The Green Man, we were still damp from the hose and speckled with polish, but it didn't matter. That kind of thing didn't bother anyone back then. Especially not on a warm evening like this. The air outside was still thick with summer, and you could hear the hum of insects somewhere just beyond the glow of the car park lamps.

We pushed through the door and into the pub's low ceiling and golden light. The smell hit first — old wood, warm beer, a faint trace of cigarette smoke clinging to the corners of every wall.

We were knackered, but our pockets were heavy.
And that made all the difference.

You carry yourself differently when you've got money in your back pocket at seventeen.
Not arrogant — just loose, confident, maybe even generous.
And we were.

We bought our first round, found a booth near the window, and let the weight of the day ease off our shoulders. Two pints in, we were laughing again. Not at anything in particular — just the kind of laugh that's born from nothing more than good company and the knowledge that you've earned tonight.

And then they showed up.

Girls from school — familiar faces, different somehow in this setting. Grown-up all of a sudden, like the glow from the beer pumps had softened them into something cinematic.

Donna was there — black hair, wide smile, sharp wit. She always had a thing for me.
So did her best mate, Debbie. Blonde. Beautiful. The kind of girl who could undo you with one look, but never made you feel like you had to impress her.
And a couple of others who barely took their eyes off Darren all night. Not that we blamed them.

They didn't plan on staying long — just came in to "say hi." But a couple of free drinks and some flirty back-and-forth later, and they were still at our table, giggling at our stories, playfully nudging shoulders, whispering things meant to be half-heard.

That night, we weren't just the lads who washed cars.
We were something more.
We were generous. Charming. *Interesting*.

And they noticed.

There was something about that feeling — that rare alignment of confidence, youth, attention — that made you feel like maybe the world really was yours, even just for one night.

By the time last orders were called, the girls were flushed and laughing, finishing their drinks before slipping out into the dark with long goodbyes and quick glances over shoulders. Whatever affection they'd shown us that night… it had been fully, warmly reciprocated.

Darren and I were left standing at the bar, grinning like we'd just won a trophy no one else knew was up for grabs.

We stepped out into the quiet night, just the two of us again.

The plan was already set — back to his place, fire up the Amiga, Speedball 2 on the screen, maybe a bag of chips on the walk if the chippy lights were still on.

It had been a perfect evening.
Golden.

One of those nights that feels full but light, like it fits perfectly in the palm of your memory.

You never know when it's going to be the last one like that.

Chapter Three – The House That Had Everything

The chippy was shut by the time we passed it, glowing dark and quiet. No surprise — it was pushing closing time. Still, we joked about breaking in for a last bag of chips and a pickled egg before turning toward the long, shadowed lane that led back to Darren's house.

The air had cooled, but the warmth from the pub still hung around our shoulders. Our pockets were lighter. Our smiles weren't.

We got back to his place and headed straight upstairs — nobody was home yet. The rest of the house echoed silence and possibility.

Darren's bedroom wasn't just a bedroom.
It was a world.

Big enough to be its own flat, it held two beds, a multi-gym weight machine, free weights on the floor, a huge wardrobe that stretched along one wall like something from a manor house, and of course — his computer. The Commodore Amiga was already humming with potential by the time we collapsed into our chairs, cracked open a can, and fired up *Speedball 2*.

There was more to his room, too — always more.

One side of the wardrobe had a secret panel that, if pushed just right, opened into a hidden passageway. It wound through the bones of the house, a hollow artery that led to other bedrooms, other secrets. There was even a ladder in there, leading up into a private loft space that felt untouched by adults or rules.

Every time I visited, Darren showed me something new — something clever, hidden, and impossible. I couldn't help but admire the way his world seemed to expand with every visit, like I was discovering a place I wasn't meant to be in, but never wanted to leave

It felt like living inside a film — and Darren was the lead character, holding the golden ticket to a life that seemed destined for greatness. I was just lucky to be there, watching it unfold.

I loved that house. Fell for it instantly, first time I stepped foot inside. Not just because of what was in it — but what it represented. Freedom. Potential. A life with space and power and *paths*. I always believed Darren was going somewhere big. Honestly, I thought he'd be a millionaire by the time he was thirty. Maybe he'd offer me a decent job one day. Not out of pity — out of loyalty. I'd always been there.

But that wasn't on the cards.
Neither of us knew it yet.

That night, though — that night was still golden.

We played games. Laughed about the girls at the pub. Debated which one fancied who and who would've kissed who if the night had gone on a bit longer. There was a rhythm to it. Two best mates in a world that, just for now, felt like it would never break.

Then we heard the front door crash open downstairs.

Laughter. Heavy footsteps. Bottles clinking. Voices full of bravado.

Steve and Johnny.

Darren just grinned and shook his head.

    "They're pissed again."

We ignored the first shout. Then the second. Laughed a little louder, hoping they'd get the hint.

But we heard them coming. Up the stairs. Footsteps clumsy but determined.

Moments later, the door burst open.
And the whole night changed direction.

Chapter Four – Into the Ditch

he door flew open with a bang, like someone had kicked it straight out of a dream.

Steve and Johnny burst into Darren's room, drunk and electric, full of laughter and hunger. They barely made it through the door before someone shouted about a Chinese.

"Proper one tonight," Johnny said, wiping his face. "Big orders, lads."

The plan sounded great — until reality kicked in.

Three phone calls later, Johnny's face dropped.

> "Nowhere delivers this late."

Silence. Frustration.

And then:

> "I'll drive — come on."

He said it like it was no big deal.

No one questioned it. No one stopped to weigh the risk. Shoes forgotten. Shirts still off. Warm from drink and sun and youth.
They followed him out.

Johnny took the wheel of the Fiesta.
Steve up front.
Darren in the back right.
Alan in the back left.

The car started. The road ahead was narrow, black, flanked by deep six-foot ditches and hedgerows closing in tight.

They pulled away with nervous excitement still clinging to them.
The chat was light. What to order. Who was paying.
Then headlights appeared behind them.

Johnny checked the mirror.

"Old bill."

He floored it.

The engine screamed.

Thirty.
Fifty.
Seventy.
Ninety.

The world outside became a smear. The car wasn't hugging the bends — it was wrestling them.

And then — **for Alan, time changed.**

It didn't just slow.
It unfolded.

The road wasn't moving fast anymore — it was moving with him.
Like reality had hit **quarter-speed.**

Everyone else later said it was over in a flash.

Not for Alan.

Every detail became high-definition.
His head turned to the right — slowly — and he caught a glimpse of Darren. Still. Frozen. Almost calm.

Then, just past Darren's shoulder, Alan saw it happen.

The rear right wheel sheared off completely.
Snapped free from its bolts and **flew** — clean over the car — vanishing into the black like a coin tossed into the night.

Alan turned forward. He saw the bend coming.

Johnny was still trying to steer — but it was too late.

The car wasn't turning. It was drifting.

Alan understood immediately.
We're going in.

And then they did.

The Fiesta dropped into the ditch **nose-first**.
Bang.

The crash came in waves — metal bending, glass bursting.
But Alan didn't scream. Didn't panic.
He was… calm.

Not numb. Not dissociating.
Aware.
Laser-focused.

His head smashed through the side window.
The wind came rushing in like a roar from another world.

He leaned away from the now open frame, **knowing** instinctively that if he got pulled out, he'd be snapped in half.

He saw Darren's head slam into the opposite window.
He saw Steve go clean through the windscreen.
He saw the shards of safety glass — **hundreds of them** — fan outward in slow motion like a shattered galaxy, flying straight at his face.

He **closed his eyes**.

Not in fear — but in control.

The car came to rest upside down, silent, ticking. Smoke. Steam. Glass on skin.

Alan opened his eyes. Time resumed.

He pressed on the back windscreen — and somehow, it fell out whole.

He crawled into the nettles, chest-deep, barefoot.

No pain.

He turned and pulled Darren out. Darren was shaken, breathing hard, but alive.

Alan went back in.

Steve's legs were still inside, his head outside the windscreen. Alan pulled him back in.

Johnny was hunched over the steering wheel, chest bruised from the impact. Alan shook him.

He stirred. Groaned.

"I'm okay."

And just like that — **they all were.**

They climbed out and stood in the dark. No sirens. No headlights. Just the sound of a car approaching — maybe the one Johnny had tried to outrun.

"Split up," someone said.

They didn't argue. They ran.

Alan sprinted barefoot through the night, every step a shock to the system, but inside he felt… nothing. Just clarity. He could still see the glass in the air and the bent metal of the car in his mind all the way back to Darren's house.

Chapter Five – The Kitchen Table

Alan reached the side of the house just as Darren was arriving at the front door. They caught sight of each other through the shadows and paused, faces still carrying the weight of what had just happened.

Darren laughed, softly.

"Which way did you come?"

Alan shook his head, still catching his breath.

"I don't really know."

They both laughed. Not the nervous kind. The genuine kind — the kind that bubbles up when you realise you're alive, and for a moment, that's all that matters.

Darren unlocked the front door and they crept inside. The house was quiet. Still no sign of his parents.

Good.

They climbed the stairs like ghosts and collapsed onto their beds. No words at first. Just the hum of the Amiga still softly glowing in the corner, and the sound of their own breathing.

They stared at the ceiling.

Minutes passed before Alan broke the silence.

"We should've died in that crash, Daz."

Darren turned his head, looked at him for a moment, then nodded.

"Yeah… I'm amazed we didn't."

They spoke in hushed voices about it — the speed, the ditch, the impossible survival. No drama. No exaggeration. Just quiet truth hanging in the air between two mates who'd been through something that didn't make sense.

Then they heard it — a key in the front door.

Footsteps. Voices.

Johnny and Steve.

Alan and Darren rushed downstairs, suddenly wide awake again.

Steve and Johnny were already in the kitchen when they got there, sitting at the big oak table like they'd just finished a normal night out. They didn't look hurt. Just wide-eyed. Shell-shocked.

Alan and Darren pulled out chairs and sat down.

No one spoke.

Four lads. One kitchen.
Stillness.

They sat in silence, just looking at each other, eyes bouncing from face to face like they were waiting for permission to speak.

After a while — maybe five minutes, maybe less — Alan started laughing.

Not a chuckle. Not a fake laugh.
A proper, gut-wrenching, breath-stealing laugh.

It broke the room open.

Darren joined in. Then Steve. Even Johnny cracked a grin and followed — chest aching, but laughing with them.

It wasn't nervous laughter.

It was *relief*. It was the absurdity of it all.
It was the only reaction that made any sense.

When they finally calmed down, wiping tears from their eyes, Steve turned to Darren.

"You alright?"

Darren nodded.

"Couple scratches, but yeah."

Steve pointed to Johnny, who was cradling his chest with one hand.

"He might've cracked a rib."

Johnny nodded slowly, confirming it with a tight-lipped smile.

Then Steve looked at Alan.

"What about you, Al?"

Alan paused.

Something shifted in his face — like he was still sorting it all out.

"Time slowed down for me," he said.

They all looked at him.

"What do you mean?" Darren asked.

"I mean... *really* slowed down. Quarter-speed, like watching it all unfold from outside myself. I saw the wheel snap. Saw it fly over the car. I saw every piece of glass. My head went through the window. Wind rushed in. I leaned away, thinking

> if I got sucked out I'd be dead. I saw Darren hit his window. I saw Steve go through the windscreen. Every second felt like a minute."

They were silent.

Alan looked at each of them in turn.

> "Did that happen to any of you?"

Three heads shook.

> "Nah," Steve said. "It was over in a flash."

But they kept looking at him. Curious. Maybe even a little spooked.

So Alan kept going.
He told them how he'd crawled out barefoot and stood on the rear windscreen, which shattered beneath his weight.
How he stood in nettles.
How he'd pulled them out, one by one.

And now, in the bright kitchen light, he stood up and looked down at himself properly for the first time.

No cuts.
No bruises.
Not even dirt on his skin.

He lifted his feet and showed them.

> "Look. Nothing."

No one said a word.

They just stared. Not doubting him — not exactly — but struggling to take it in.

Eventually, someone suggested they go back upstairs. Hide away before the parents got back.

It was a good call.

They scattered like kids caught red-handed.

Alan and Darren slipped back into the sanctuary of that oversized bedroom and collapsed again — only this time, the games stayed off. The room was dark, quiet. Their voices were barely more than whispers.

They talked for hours. Trying to make sense of what had happened. Of why they were still alive. Of *how* they were still alive.

Alan had shared a theory with Darren — one that unsettled them both.
He said he was convinced they should've died in the crash. All of them.
But they didn't.

Now, he wondered: *What if everyone has a predetermined expiration date?*
A fixed moment you can't outrun or delay — no matter what.

He even suggested testing it.

Darren shifted uncomfortably, his expression darkening. "Drop it," he said. "It's getting morbid."

Then came the front door.

Voices. Laughter.

Darren's parents. Home at last.
Nothing out of the ordinary. They hadn't seen the car. They didn't know.

Alan and Darren looked at each other, then kept whispering.

Another hour passed.

Then — the doorbell.

Barbara, Darren's mom, answered it.

A voice Alan didn't recognise at first. Then it clicked.

Johnny's mom.

> "Is Johnny here?"

Barbara called upstairs.

> "Steve! Is Johnny up there?"

> "Yeah!" came the reply.

Footsteps. Heavy. Slow.

Then **SLAP.**

Shouting.
Accusation.
Something about the police finding the car — keys still in the ignition — and knowing Johnny had been drinking.

Alan turned to Darren.

> "We should probably pretend to be asleep."

Darren nodded.

They both pulled the covers up and closed their eyes — not to rest, but to hide.

That night Alan had a dream. He was in an unfamiliar place. It was him – but he was older. Greying hair. Carrying a little more weight than before. There was a mirror but the reflection within was unclear.

A voice "This is how you die…"

For the briefest flicker of a moment, a plain, ordinary chair appeared in his dream — unremarkable, yet unmistakably final.

He woke up in shock and looked around. The room was dark. Darren was sleeping. The house was silent. It was just a dream. He closed his eyes and went back to sleep.

Chapter Six – The Corner.

othing really happened for a while after that. Life rolled on.

More college work. More car valeting on our days off. More beers. More laughs.

Only now, I was different.

Not in a way you'd spot. I still acted the same — cracked jokes, played it cool, never missed a pint.
But inside... something had shifted.

A quiet awareness. Like I'd stepped out of the current for a moment and now couldn't stop feeling the flow tugging at my ankles.

I started noticing things.

Little things.

Crossing the road and stopping for no reason, only for a car to shoot past that should've had me plastered across its bonnet.

Heading to clean a car I *thought* we were booked for — and finding broken glass on the seat, like someone had tried to break in.

Once, in the pub, some random girl I'd never met looked straight at me and said, "You've got the kind face of a ghost."

Then just laughed and walked away.

But one memory lodged itself sharper than the rest.

It was a lazy Sunday — one of those golden late afternoons where the heat had softened just enough to make it perfect. I was loafing about, probably nursing the back end of a hangover, when my old man called out from the hallway: "You want anything from the offie?"

"Yeah," I shouted back, "grab me something, Pops!"

He laughed — that warm, dry chuckle of his — and said, "Come with me, you cheeky git. You can carry the stuff."

So I went. No reason not to.

We climbed into the car, and he pulled out onto the road — nothing unusual, until I noticed his foot a bit heavier on the pedal than usual.

He was never a boy-racer, my dad. Always the steady type. But this time, there was pace. Not mad, just... noticeable.

I found my hand gripping the side of the seat. The other went up to the "oh shit" handle, like instinct.

And I could feel it. That fizz again. Like a shaken bottle of pop under the surface.

Then I felt his eyes on me.
I turned and caught his stare — deep, quiet, knowing. Like he wasn't just looking *at* me, but *through* me.

"You alright?" he asked, brow creased.

He had that gift, my Pops. Like Darren. Like some inner radar for truth. You couldn't bullshit either of them — not properly.

I laughed — too loud, too fake — and tried to shake it off. "Woah, slow down there, Sterling," I said. A joke. A nod to Moss.

He didn't laugh. Just kept looking for a second longer than was comfortable...
Then turned back to the road and eased off the gas as we came to the corner.

That corner. It worried me. We weren't even going fast, but the fear surged again.
Like a warning bell in my chest, ringing louder than the engine.

I swallowed it down. Styled out the rest of the ride like a champion.
But inside? I was shook.

It passed, like most things do. But it stayed, too — in the way things do when they're *quietly important*.
I didn't talk about it. Didn't dwell on it.

Life carried on. I stopped noticing the oddities. Forgot the close calls.
Or told myself I had.

But not completely.

Not until the next disaster.

Chapter Seven – The Man with No Pint

It was one of those nothing Fridays.

No plans. No grand schemes. Just one of those evenings where you end up in the pub because it's Friday and what else are you going to do?

Me and Darren were already two pints in and halfway through a game of darts that neither of us was keeping proper score for. The jukebox was doing its best to play something for everyone and please no one. Somebody'd just queued up *Sandstorm* again, which Darren insisted was a "classic," despite being so jittery it made the glasses rattle.

I leaned against the bar, half-watching a group of lads in the corner throw coins at the fruit machine like it owed them money. Darren was still muttering about his last throw being sabotaged by "weird airflow" when a voice spoke from behind me.

"Your shadow's on the wrong side."

I turned.
He was already walking away.

Not old, not young. Late thirties maybe. Jeans, grey hoodie, face I didn't recognise.
But he walked like he knew where he was going. Like someone who belonged. Only… he had no drink in his hand. No pint, no glass, no nothing.

Just walked straight out the pub like he'd popped in to drop off a message from the universe.

I blinked, confused.

"What?" I said, mostly to myself.

Darren turned. "What?"

"Nothing." I looked back. The door was already swinging shut.
"Some bloke just said something weird and left."

"Probably someone you owe money to," Darren grinned, lining up his next dart. "Or one of your adoring fans."

I chuckled, but my skin had that cold prickle like when someone opens a fridge behind you. I didn't even know what he *meant* — "your shadow's on the wrong side"? What the hell does that even mean?

But it stuck. Like a splinter under the skin of the night.

Later, while Darren was talking bollocks with someone from his old rugby team, I went outside for a smoke I didn't really want. I stood there, watching people stagger out of taxis and into the pub like pilgrims at a temple of regret.

A girl in a red coat passed me on the way out, gave me a polite smile. I nodded.

Two people were walking down the street nearby, engaged in conversation. As they passed, I caught a snippet of their chatter — one of them said, 'I was there at 8:17.' It didn't register much at the time, just another fragment of their conversation.

Then I caught my own shadow on the pavement.

It was long. Too long. The light wasn't *that* bright behind me. I stepped forward. The shadow twitched — not in sync. Just off. Like it moved a heartbeat before I did.

I rubbed my eyes. Laughed at myself.
Too much ale. Not enough chips.

Still, I stubbed the cig early and went back in.

Nothing else happened. Not that night.

We finished our pints. Took the piss out of the quiz machine.
Said goodbye like it was just another night — because it was.

But walking home, I couldn't shake the feeling.
Not dread. Not even fear, really.

Just a question.

Was something watching me?

Chapter Eight – Not Where I Left Them

arren had gone off on some ski trip with his college mates — white slopes, expensive gear, overpriced lager, the lot.

I didn't go. Couldn't afford it. Didn't want to anyway.

Instead, I stayed back in Walmley, house-sitting while my parents were away for a few days. Just me, a fridge full of leftovers, and the old family home. Cosy in a way — familiar creaks, familiar smells, the low hum of the boiler like a cat purring through the pipes.

And most importantly: **time**.
Time to make something.

I'd gotten it into my head I was going to surprise Darren. Blow his mind.
A full-blown fantasy RPG made in *DarkBASIC*. Something gritty and pixelated, like the love child of Dungeon Master and Eye of the Beholder.
Just text, music, mood, and imagination.

The screen glowed in that way old CRTs do when you're the only one awake in the house. I'd been working on dialogue trees for an hour before realising the sun had gone. I hadn't put the lights on — just the monitor and the blue-white cast across the wallpaper behind me. That kind of light made shadows stretch long and thin across the room. Familiar shadows.

Until one wasn't.

I froze. There were two shadows on the wall.

Mine.

And a second.

I turned, heart spiking. Nothing. Just the empty room. I stared for a while, trying to logic my way out of it.
Maybe a coat on the back of the door?

The monitor reflecting weird?
Maybe my own shadow had split from two light sources?

Whatever it was, by the time I turned back, it was gone.

Still, it left that humming in my chest. Like a string pulled taut and vibrating in my ribcage.

Later that night, I went to bed — finally — with the kind of brain that won't shut off. That coding buzz where you keep seeing numbers and logic in your dreams.
I laid there in the dark, watching the reflections shift on the ceiling from the streetlights outside. At some point, I must've drifted off.

I dreamed of hallways.

Endless, flickering corridors.
Like a hospital. Or a bunker.
Cold, tiled floors. Fluorescent lights that blinked just fast enough to set your teeth on edge.
And footsteps behind me that never quite caught up.

I woke with a jolt. Heart racing. Dry mouth.
Had no idea what time it was. The house was dead quiet — too quiet. Not even the boiler purring.

I shuffled downstairs to grab some water, still half in the dream. As I passed the mirror in the hallway, I paused. Something about it looked off.

It was normal. My reflection was normal.

But I stepped left — and in the mirror, I stepped right.

Only... there was a split second where it didn't. Where the reflection *didn't keep up*. Just lagged a heartbeat.

Then snapped back.

I stared, water forgotten.
Then did something I'd never done before.

I waved at myself.

And my reflection waved back...
Just slightly out of sync.
Like it had only *just remembered* that's what it was supposed to do.

In the morning, I couldn't find my car keys.

I'd left them on the kitchen table. I *knew* I had. I always did.

But they weren't there.

I searched the counter, the sideboard, my coat. Even checked the fridge, because I'd done that once before when I was half-cut. Nothing.

It wasn't until I went upstairs — no reason, just a weird pull — that I found them.

On the windowsill of the spare bedroom.

A room I hadn't been in.

I stood there for a full minute, staring at them like they were ticking.

No one else had been in the house.

I picked them up slowly, like they might burn.

That evening, I went back to the mirror.

Tried it again.

Nothing. Normal.

Almost.

As I turned to walk away, I swear — *swear* — I saw myself stay put for just a second longer.

Watching me.

Chapter Nine – Back from the Snow

arren came back from his ski trip the way Darren always came back from anything — with a sunburnt nose, two less t-shirts, and at least five stories he couldn't finish without grinning like an idiot.

He dumped his bag by the door, collapsed onto my sofa, and let out a noise somewhere between a sigh and a growl.

"British weather's shite," he declared, like it was news.

"Welcome home, travel king," I said, handing him a brew. "How's the knee?"

"Blown." He flexed it with a wince. "Too much ambition, not enough balance."

"Same could be said for your haircut."

He gave me the finger. Normal service resumed.

Later that evening, after the catch-up, the takeaway, and some channel-hopping that landed us on a rerun of *Knightmare*, I finally showed him what I'd built.

The game.

My game.

DarkBASIC in all its glory — a crude dungeon crawler with static images, text commands, and moody chip-tune music I'd stitched together in some dodgy MIDI editor.

To me, it was magic. Atmosphere. Immersion.
To Darren... well.

He leaned forward, squinted at the code for five minutes, then burst out laughing.

"Oh my *God*, mate — you could've done this in half the lines if you just used—hold on, hold on..."

He shoved me aside and cracked his knuckles over the keyboard like a pianist about to outplay Mozart. In ten minutes flat, he'd written a new engine — one that handled text prompts, image swaps, player inventory and directional logic cleaner than I'd ever dreamed.

I watched, pretending to sulk but secretly in awe. That was Darren. The bastard could *think in code*. Like his brain was wired in curly brackets.

Once he'd finished showing off, we played the new version together — taking turns typing commands, reading the narration aloud in overly dramatic voices.

"You enter the hall of whispers," I boomed. "The air is cold. You hear faint breathing."

"Sexy," Darren replied.

I grinned. "There's a door to the north and a strange mirror to the east."

"Ooh, mirrors again," he said. "That your new kink?"

I said nothing. Just smiled a bit too tightly.

But then — just as we were getting cocky with it — the weird happened.

We typed the command:

> LOOK IN MIRROR

And the game responded with a line neither of us had written.

> You are being watched. 8:17.

I froze. Darren frowned.

"The hell?"

I leaned forward. "That's not part of the—"

Before I could finish, another line appeared.

> He sees you now.

No typing. Just… there.

Darren backed away slightly. "Is this one of your add-ins? Like a triggered response thing?"

"I swear," I said, "I didn't write that."

He stared at me, then at the code window. "Mate. The editor's clean. There's no text file. There's nothing calling those strings. What the Hell is 8:17?"

I reopened the script. Searched every function. Nothing.

The words were just… not there. Anywhere.

Then the lights flickered.

Just once. But it was enough to make us both sit still. Breathing shallow.

The game froze.

The screen turned black.

Then a single line of text appeared in white:

> He knows your names.

And then it crashed. Back to desktop. No error. No warning.

Just gone.

We stared in silence. The room suddenly felt too big. Too cold. Too *aware*.

Darren was the first to speak.

"I don't like that," he said, quiet now. "I don't like that at all."

I looked at the dark screen.
"Me neither."

That night, we didn't talk much. Didn't put the TV back on. We sat around pretending to scroll through our phones, waiting for bedtime to make the silence normal again.

But I knew.
Darren knew.
And now whatever *it* was — knew too.

Chapter Ten – The Bridge Test

Alan had been wrestling with a theory for some time — chewing it over, bouncing it back and forth with Darren.

Darren didn't like it. Not one bit.
But Alan insisted it was worth exploring.

Death has a design.
Each of us has a fixed time.
Final. Inescapable.
You can't go before it, and you can't go after it.

And if that were true… then something — *something* — would have to intervene every time death was near.

That's what led to the tests.

They'd been discussing it for weeks — the strange messages in the code.
Who was watching them?
Who knew their names?
And what the hell was the significance of *8:17*?

Alan kept pushing his theory about expiration dates, while Darren — growing more frustrated by the day — insisted Alan was losing it.

The patterns. The close calls. The idea that maybe — just maybe — Alan couldn't die until a certain time. Until 8:17. This year? 10 years from now? He wasn't sure.

It sounded insane. But it was harder and harder to ignore.

"I need to know for sure," Alan said, pacing Darren's bedroom like a man half-mad with theory. "All these things — they weren't just luck."

Darren sat on the edge of the bed, frowning. "So what, we run some tests?"

Alan stopped. "Yeah. But this time, something real. Something I shouldn't be able to survive."

Darren raised an eyebrow. "Define 'real.'"

Alan turned to him, face set. 'I can't swim well enough to get myself out of this situation, so I should die, right? If I throw myself into a river off a bridge, for instance?"

Darren didn't reply immediately.

That night, they stood at the edge of a high bridge just outside town. The water below was dark and wide, its surface slow-moving but heavy with cold. Rust streaked the iron rails. Nobody came out here after dark — not unless they were serious.

Alan stood on the stone lip, trainers inches from the edge.

"This is mad," Darren said quietly. "You know that?"

Alan nodded. "Yup."

"You're not a strong swimmer. That's not theory — that's fact."

"That's the point."

Darren crossed his arms, watching him carefully. "If it looks like you're not coming up, I'm in after you."

Alan glanced back. "I know. That's why I asked you to come."

He turned forward again, heart pounding. The water looked further away now than when they'd arrived. He took a breath that didn't feel deep enough.

Then he jumped.

The cold hit like violence.
It slammed into him like a wall — breathtaking, literal.
His lungs seized. The scream he never got to make died in his throat.
The world turned to black water and pain.

He sank fast — too fast.
The weight of his clothes dragged him down, his trainers offering no fight. His arms flailed instinctively, but his brain was already shutting down rational thought.
Up was down. Down was everywhere.
He spun, twisted, kicked at nothing.

Water rushed into his ears. The pressure built behind his eyes. Panic lit up every nerve.
He opened his mouth to scream — a reflex — and the river poured in.

No!
He clamped his mouth shut, coughing inside his own head, chest jerking. He thrashed violently, trying to kick upward, but the surface was gone. Lost to the dark.

He couldn't see. Couldn't breathe. Couldn't think.

His body began to betray him — limbs slowing, movements losing strength.
Something primal screamed inside him to fight, but everything else whispered: *Let go.*

Then — something.
A blur of light above.
Was it the surface? Moonlight? His brain playing tricks?

He clawed toward it, every movement a brutal act of will.
His chest convulsed again — a spasm. His lips parted.

Water surged in.

His mind began to split. Time bent and stretched. His thoughts fractured into flashes:
A young boy running in a garden.
His dad's voice.
The smell of rain on warm tarmac.

His mom's face — concerned, watching him like she knew he was struggling.
Then nothing. Blank white static.

But something inside him wasn't done.
A spark. A pulse. A reason.
He kicked once more, blindly — and burst through the surface.

He gasped, but half of it was a choke. He retched and sucked at the air like it was solid gold. His arms slapped at the water, trying to stay up.

He was slipping under again. Dizzy. Weak.
But this time he saw the branch — half-submerged, mossy, cruel.

He clawed for it, missed. Tried again. Caught it.
His arms screamed. His grip faltered.

Then — hands.

Rough, solid, human hands.
Grabbing his jacket. Locking on.

Darren.

Pulling like hell.

Dragging him through the mud, over the roots, onto the grass.

Alan collapsed in a heaving, soaked mess. He curled onto his side and vomited river water, bile, air, and panic all at once.

His lungs burned. His limbs shook uncontrollably. His heartbeat jackhammered in his ears.

Darren dropped beside him, panting hard. "Jesus Christ, Alan…"

Alan coughed, groaned, tried to speak — couldn't.

"You absolute idiot," Darren said, voice shaking. "What the fuck were you thinking?"

Alan managed to croak, "I made it."

"*Barely.*" Darren was soaked to the waist from leaning in. "You were *gone*, man. You were under forever."

"I should've died," Alan rasped. "I felt it… I was… gone."

Darren looked at him, something raw flickering behind his eyes.

"I was this close," he whispered, holding his fingers up. "You didn't come up when you should have. I was already stepping up. I was going in."

Alan turned his head, still gasping, pale as milk. "It wasn't me. I didn't make it up… something pulled me."

Darren stared at him.

Then looked away.

"Inconclusive," he muttered. "You swam. Maybe just enough."

Alan rolled onto his back, water dripping from his hair, stars spinning overhead.

"No," he whispered. "It's beginning."

Chapter Eleven – Traffic and Chaos

Time moved on.

Darren got sharper. Alan just got stuck.

Darren had aced his exams — no surprise to anyone who knew him — and moved into halls at Nottingham Uni, studying Computer Science. He lived off Beeston Road, just past the student union and the kebab place with the dodgy signage. He talked about algorithms, recursion, architecture — all that big-brain stuff.

Alan, on the other hand, bounced between warehouse jobs. Pallets, forklifts, cold storage. Places that smelled of shrink wrap and despair. He told people it was "just for now," but that now kept dragging on.

They still talked. Still met up. Darren would take the train home some weekends, or Alan would grab a lift up to Nottingham, crash on the futon in Darren's shoebox-sized room.

But Alan had changed.

More distant. Obsessed. Still locked into the theory like it owed him something. He'd stopped calling it a hunch. Now he called it *proof* waiting to happen.

And that's why they were standing by the crossing on Beeston Road.

Darren watched as Alan stepped off the curb.

"Al…" he said, quietly. "You sure?"

Alan looked over his shoulder, calm. "No. But that's the point."

The road was madness — lunchtime traffic snarling in both directions, buses swerving, cyclists weaving. Alan picked his moment and stepped out, right into the middle of it all.

A horn blared instantly. A car — dark grey, mid-sized, something reliable — was barrelling toward him. The driver slammed the brakes but it was already too late. There was no space. No time. Alan didn't move.

This is it, he thought. This is where I find out.

And then the world shifted.

From the left — completely unexpected — another car came screaming out of nowhere. Sirens howling behind it. A police chase. The fleeing car ploughed through the intersection and **slammed into the oncoming car**, metal folding like paper, glass exploding into the air like fireworks.

The impact knocked both vehicles sideways — away from Alan.

He didn't flinch. Just stood there, heart hammering.

Screams. Shouts. A second later, Darren was at his side, grabbing his jacket, yanking him back toward the pavement.

A body was slumped across the wheel of the car that should have hit Alan. Blood smeared across the airbag. One of the officers ran up, radio barking. Another looked straight at Alan — then moved past him, toward the wreckage.

They didn't stop him. Didn't question him.

Someone had just **died in his place**.

Alan and Darren stood in silence, the traffic around them in frozen chaos.

Alan's hands trembled, but his eyes were clear.

He turned to Darren.

"This isn't theory anymore."

That night, back in his dorm, Darren sat staring at his screen. Something didn't sit right.

He'd been working on a simple input parser earlier — a uni assignment — when he noticed something buried deep in the codebase. Not his work. Not from a library.

A line, embedded like a virus.

A. Carter – 8:17

He deleted it. Hit save.

Closed the project. Reopened it.

The line was back.

He tried deleting it again — a different file this time. New project. Fresh start.

Still came back.

    "A. Carter – 8:17"

But now… there was more.

"Year unknown."

He sat back, heart sinking.

How the hell did it get there?

And why couldn't he get rid of it?

Chapter Twelve – The Real Tests Begin

They met up a few days later — the air still thick with what happened on Beeston Road.

Alan had barely touched his pint. He wasn't jittery, he wasn't bragging — he was thinking. Turning something over in his head like a stone he couldn't quite let go of.

Darren knew that look.

"I've got an idea for the next test," Alan finally said, quiet.

Darren slammed his glass down. "Someone died because of your last test, Al!"

Alan didn't flinch. "I know. That's why this one's different. It's clean. Logical. There's no way anyone else gets hurt."

Darren gave him a look — not angry, just tired. "You're not hearing yourself anymore."

Alan leaned in. "Listen… I stand in an open courtyard. You drop a brick from a fixed height. No crowds. No traffic. No interference. Either I die… or we finally get our answer."

Darren shook his head, but it wasn't a no. "You've thought this through."

"Every angle."

A pause. Darren sighed. "You'd better be right."

They met behind an abandoned factory unit — just outside Long Eaton. Wide-open space. Alan stood below an old service ladder, concrete beneath him. A single brick in Darren's hand, trembling slightly.

Alan looked up, calm.

Darren leaned out, voice barely audible. "You're still okay with this?"

Alan gave a thumbs up. "Do it."

Darren counted down. "Three… two… one…"

He dropped it.

The brick fell fast — a clean line, direct.

And then, **out of nowhere**, a pigeon swooped down — mad, wild, fast — and clipped the brick mid-air.

The bird took the hit.

The brick veered off to the side and shattered harmlessly on the concrete.

The bird hit the ground near Alan with a sickening thud. One wing twitched. Then stopped.

Alan froze.

Darren climbed down, pale, jaw clenched.

They stood over the broken thing together, watching it bleed quietly into the dust.

Neither spoke for a long time.

Eventually, Darren said, "That shouldn't have happened."

Alan nodded, eyes distant. "But it did."

He crouched next to the bird — not touching it, just looking.

"It's like the world won't let me go," he said. "It finds something. Anything. To take instead."

Darren crouched too. "I wanted this one to be safe. I thought it was."

"I did too."

They looked at each other, and for the first time since it all began, they both **believed** the same thing.

Alan stood, brushing dust off his jeans.

"Where there should be death," he said softly, "there will always be death."

Darren nodded, eyes still on the bird.

"Just not yours."

Chapter Thirteen – The Exchange

They agreed it would be the last one.

Not because they were scared, not even because they were sure — but because they were tired. Theories could only stretch so far before they snapped. And if the universe had rules, then surely it would show its hand one last time.

"If nothing happens," Darren said, "we walk away from this."

Alan nodded. "And if something does?"

Darren didn't answer.

At 21:00 they drove out to the edge of an old, disused airfield — long overgrown, rusted fencing leaning into weeds, tarmac split with cracks like veins. No cameras. No one watching. Just sky and wind and the low throb of tension building in their chests.

Alan stood at the far end of the runway.

Darren sat behind the wheel of his clapped-out Ford, hands gripping tight, engine idling.

"You ready?" he asked over the radio.

Alan pressed the button on his own walkie-talkie. "I'm ready."

Darren took a breath, dropped it into gear, and floored it.

The car screamed forward, tyres spitting dust, speed climbing fast. Alan didn't move. Didn't blink. He was bracing for the moment — the true test. Nothing between him and a half-tonne of steel.

And then the wheel twisted.

Hard. Like a hand yanked it sideways.

Darren shouted — a guttural noise, not even a word — as the car lurched left, skidded, and spun. Tyres howled. The car flashed past Alan with inches to spare. The air around him changed with the speed of it — a blur of metal and noise.

Then the car tipped.

Rolled once.

Twice.

Three times.

Came to a crunching stop against the edge of a long-dead perimeter fence.

Alan stood, motionless.

Darren kicked the door open, coughing, shaken, but uninjured.

No blood. No broken bones.

Just silence.

They ended up in the pub later, still running on adrenaline. Same place they'd gone to after everything important. It was nearly empty, lit low, just the murmur of glasses and one guy in the corner swearing at the fruit machine.

Darren nursed a whisky. Alan stuck to water.

"I didn't move the wheel," Darren said, for the third time.

Alan nodded slowly. "I believe you."

"It was like… something took it from me. Not like a slip. Not like nerves. Just gone. Wrenched. Yanked."

Alan stirred his drink, staring into it like it might offer answers.

"You didn't even flinch," Darren said.

"I felt it coming," Alan replied. "I knew it wouldn't hit me."

They sat in silence for a while, the space between them heavy with everything that wasn't being said.

Then a voice broke the quiet.

"Alan? Darren?"

They both turned.

A figure approached from the bar — tall, stocky, red hoodie, fading buzzcut. Familiar face, older now, softer around the edges.

"Duncan?" Darren said, eyebrows rising.

"No way," Alan muttered, standing to shake his hand. "It's been years."

"Yeah, man," Duncan smiled, then it faltered. "Hey… uh… did you hear about Donna?"

The name froze the air.

Alan blinked. "No. What about her?"

Duncan looked between them, like maybe they *should* have known already. He rubbed the back of his neck, stepped in closer.

"Mate… she got hit. A drunk driver. Last night."

Alan's stomach turned cold.

Darren's glass stopped halfway to his mouth.

Duncan nodded slowly. "Crossing the road on her way to meet a few people from school last night around 9 o'clock. By the chippy on King Edward's. They said it was instant. She didn't stand a chance."

Alan sat back down, slow, eyes glassing over.

Darren stared at the table, jaw clenched.

Duncan let out a shaky breath. "I'm sorry. I thought you'd know."

They nodded, barely hearing him.

After a few awkward seconds, Duncan gave them a soft "take care," and walked away.

Outside, the air was sharp with evening chill. They sat on a bench out front, staring at nothing.

"She died," Alan said.

"Yeah," Darren replied.

"At the same time," Alan said. "As the test."

"Yeah."

Alan rubbed his face, eyes red. "I thought I'd planned it right. No traffic. No chance of anyone else…"

"You did," Darren said. "But it doesn't matter."

Alan looked at him.

Darren stared straight ahead.

"Where there should be death," he said quietly, "there will always be death."

Alan said nothing.

Behind them, the pub door creaked closed.

A pigeon took flight from the roof, flapping upward into the darkening sky.

Neither of them moved.

Chapter Fourteen – The Chair Appears

Alan always said the garden saved his dad.

After his mom passed, it had become his whole world — all neat borders and military precision. Tulips, peonies, rose arches that framed the lawn like a cathedral nave. In the centre: the fish pond. Big. Deep. Originally meant to be a swimming pool for "the kids" — but English weather had different ideas.

Instead, it became home to a dozen Koi.

And one of them, Flloyd, was a legend.

Massive. Moody. And obsessed with sunbathing. He'd launch himself from the pond onto the warm slabs, lie there like a little orange crocodile, then flip back in with a sploosh that echoed round the garden.

Alan used to joke he was solar-powered.

Even now, years later, Alan found peace just standing at the patio doors, sipping tea, watching that mad fish do his thing. It made things feel simple again.

Until the chair turned.

He was in the kitchen, waiting for the kettle to finish screaming, when he noticed it — one of the dining chairs, the one closest to the double doors, had twisted away from the table. Just slightly. Like someone had pulled it out to sit... but hadn't.

It faced the garden.

Alan frowned. Walked over. Pushed it back under the table.

Didn't think much of it.

Then the phone rang in the hallway — landline, old-school, still clinging to the wall like it was 1995. He answered it.

Wrong number.

Hung up. Walked back into the kitchen.

And stopped dead.

The chair was in the middle of the floor.

Not turned.

Moved.

All the way out. Centre of the room. Just sitting there. Watching him.

Alan's breath hitched.

He looked around. Nothing. Empty house. Quiet.

He stared at the chair. Then walked over, slow, cautious, heart ticking up like a second hand.

He put it back.

Tucked it in tightly this time.

Didn't make tea.

Just went upstairs.

That night, his dreams came hard and strange.

Donna was standing at a crossing. She looked older — same face, different hair. Brighter. But her smile kept flickering like an old film reel.

He tried to call out to her. His mouth didn't work.

The sky changed colour. Blue, then amber. Then blood red.

A car appeared in the distance. Silent. Fast.

Donna turned.

She wasn't Donna anymore.

Then—

Impact.

Screech.

Darkness.

Alan woke with a jolt.

The bedroom was freezing.

He sat up, drenched in sweat. Blinked blearily around the room.

And saw it.

The chair.

At the foot of his bed.

Same chair. Dining room.

Not turned now.

Just *there*.

Like it had always been.

Watching.

Waiting.

Alan didn't scream.

Didn't move.

He just stared at it.

    "Where there should be death…" he whispered.

And the chair said nothing.

Chapter Fifteen – Something's Watching

The computer lab buzzed low with ancient fans and CRT hum. Every screen glowed green-on-black — a digital fantasy stitched together by text and code. Discworld MUD. Their old haunt.

Alan's thief character, Lokie, was lagging behind Darren's Tadpole by leagues, but it didn't matter. They moved as a pair — stealing things, dodging guards, creeping through dungeons made from lines of code and imagination.

They didn't talk much while playing. Just the occasional grin, or muttered comment when one of them messed up a command and got walloped by a rabid hedge-wizard.

It was their escape.

For a few hours, everything else disappeared — the tests, the deaths, the weight of it all.

When they finally logged out, the world felt quieter. Emptier. Realer.

They left the building, jackets zipped up, the chill of Nottingham night wrapping around them like a damp blanket.

Campus was mostly deserted.

The orange glow of the sodium lamps stretched long shadows across the cracked paving stones. In the distance, the cathedral spire cut into the sky like a knife, silhouetted by cloudlight.

They walked in silence for a bit, heading back toward Darren's shared house off Derby Road. The kind of silence that only two old friends can wear comfortably.

Alan was mid-sentence about a quest they'd never finished when he stopped.

His voice just… died.

Darren followed his gaze.

Someone was walking toward them.

Far off at first. A silhouette. Hoodie up. No bag. No drink.

Just walking.

Closer. Steady pace. Not hurrying.

Alan froze.

Darren narrowed his eyes. "Who the hell is that?"

The man walked right past them.

No eye contact. No nod.

But just as he passed, his head turned just slightly — not enough to show his face, but enough that they heard him speak.

"Wrong path again, Lokie."

Soft. Calm. Like it wasn't meant to frighten — just to *remind*.

Then he was gone.

Alan spun.

So did Darren.

The man was gone.

The path behind them was empty.

No footfalls. No rustle. Just silence.

Alan stared into the dark.

Darren looked at him. "What the fuck was that?"

Alan didn't answer.

He was pale.

Still staring at where the man had been.

Eventually, he spoke.

> "That's him. The man from the pub. The one who said my shadow was on the wrong side."

Darren looked shaken for the first time in a long time.

"What did he just say?"

Alan's voice was quiet. "Wrong path again, Lokie."

Darren blinked. "Lokie… your thief?"

Alan nodded.

Darren turned full toward him. "There's no way he could know that."

They stood in silence again, the sodium lamps humming above them.

Darren folded his arms, rubbing at the back of his neck.

"What does he mean — wrong path again?"

Alan didn't answer right away.

Then:

"Maybe I'm not supposed to be testing it anymore. Maybe I'm not supposed to be fighting it."

Darren exhaled sharply. "Or maybe someone — or something — is trying to warn you."

Alan looked toward the dark again.

"Then why does it feel like it's already too late?"

Chapter Sixteen – Darren's Discovery

The spider was coming along.

Darren had spent the last six hours tweaking the movement code — adjusting the limb articulation so it didn't just crawl like a wind-up toy, but moved with that horrible, hypnotic grace spiders had. All eight legs shifted in calculated pulses. Back legs wide for balance. Front ones twitching slightly. It was… beautiful. And horrifying.

Exactly what his professor wanted.

He leaned back in his desk chair, fingers clicking absently on the mouse, replaying the latest simulation frame by frame. The 3D model skittered over a grey test grid like it owned the place.

He smiled. Briefly.

Then something on the console output caught his eye.

>   A.CARTER – 14 MAY 2043 – 08:17

He frowned.

The text wasn't part of the simulation. Not part of the spider control logic. Just a string dumped between logs. A rogue entry.

He opened the codebase. Searched every line.

Nothing.

He ran a recursive grep. Still nothing.

He deleted the entry from the output manually. Saved. Recompiled.

Reran the test.

It was gone.

Good.

He pressed play.

The spider moved exactly as it should.

Then at the very end of the test…

    A.CARTER – 14 MAY 2043 – 08:17

Back again.

Same font. Same line number. Same exact timestamp.

Darren sat up straighter. Leaned in. Hit pause.

No function should be outputting that. It wasn't in memory. It wasn't coming from the model. It wasn't even encoded in his data files.

He went deeper. Cleared cache. Deleted and re-cloned the whole repo from scratch.

Ran it fresh.

Still there.

    A.CARTER   14 MAY 2043 – 08:17

He stared at it.

Cold sweat started to form under his shirt.

He deleted the directory entirely. Opened a blank project. Wrote two lines of hello-world code.

Ran it. This time:

Sit in the chair.

No.

No way.

He stood up, chair scraping against the floor, heart suddenly thudding against his chest like it wanted out.

He pulled the power cord from the PC.

Darkness.

Silence.

Just his breath in the dim blue of his dorm room.

He didn't sleep.

He sat at his desk with a pen and paper, scribbling possible explanations. Timestamp injection? Malware? He wasn't connected to the network. BIOS rootkit? Ghost process?

None of it made sense.

Around 3:10 AM, he sat back and stared at the note he had made of the date again.

14 May 2043.

A.Carter.

8:17.

"Sit in the chair."

That time again.

His hands were shaking slightly as he picked up his phone.

Alan's name was already at the top of the call list.

He tapped it.

Three rings. Then a groggy voice.

"'Lo?"

Darren didn't wait.

> "Al… I know when you die."

Silence on the other end.

Then:

"…what?"

> "The code keeps telling me. I've tried everything. It's not a bug. It's not random. I've deleted it. Rewritten the file. Even changed machines. It still comes back."

Alan was sitting up now. Sheets tangled around his legs.

Darren continued, voice low.

> "May fourteenth. 2043. 8:17 a.m.
> It's the chair — the one that moved. You said it moved."

Alan didn't speak.

Darren stared at the dark monitor, seeing his own reflection.

> "It's not just a pattern, Al. It's a message.
> Someone… something… wants us to know."

He paused.

"You've got eighteen years."

Click.

Silence.

Chapter Seventeen – The Cost of One Friend

He didn't sleep for a week after finding the date.

He tried. He lay there most nights staring at the ceiling, watching the shape of the room shift in the dark. The code still flickered behind his eyes. The words still sat in his mind like they'd been carved there.

    A. Carter – 14 May 2043 – 08:17

He could still see it… appearing in logs where it shouldn't exist. Coming back even when he tore the code down to its foundations. It wasn't *in* the program. It *was* the program. Or something underneath it. Something older.

At first, Darren had thought it was a message. A warning.

Now… he wasn't so sure.

It felt like *truth*. Not a threat. Not a choice. Just… inevitability.

He ran simulations in his head.

Dozens.

If he unplugged Alan from the world — took away every possible variable — could he cheat the system?

But no. That's not how it worked.

They'd learned that already.

    Where there should be death…
    There will always be death.

You could run. You could hide. You could reroute the train tracks.

But the train still came.

He sat at his desk late one night, empty Red Bull cans stacked like tiny monuments to stress, and stared at the line of code again. It wasn't glowing or moving. Just… sitting there. Waiting.

He closed his laptop.

Rubbed his face.

Then asked the question he hadn't dared voice until now:

> "What if it's not supposed to be Alan?"

The silence that followed was loud.

He leaned back in his chair.

He'd never told anyone, but he'd always assumed Alan would go first. Not out of malice. Just… Alan always *felt* fragile. Not physically. Just spiritually. Like he was born with too many windows and not enough walls.

He was the scruffy one. The one who didn't revise, didn't plan, didn't fight for the front row.

Darren was supposed to be the brilliant one.

The one with a future.

He had plans. A degree. A probable career in AI or defence or high-tier development.

He already had a job at a company that would later become Google.

He had it all.

So why... why was he even considering this?

Why was he now seriously, *rationally*, planning how to take Alan's place?

He listed it out.

Like a logic tree.

Objections:
1. **Alan's not exceptional.**
   No ambition. No roadmap. No real "spark," right?

2. **I've got everything ahead of me.**
   I could retire before I'm 40 if I play it right.

3. **There's no reason this fate should fall on me.**
   I didn't ask for this.

4. **He's not my responsibility.**
   He never has been.

But then...
The counter-arguments started rising. Unstoppable.

> "He wasn't exceptional... but he was *there*."

Every day. Every weird obsession. Every all-nighter spent playing games or talking about the shape of the universe.

> "He chose me."

When nobody else cared about coding or learning or systems, Alan leaned in with wide eyes and stupid questions and unwavering awe. He has always been there from the age of 5. That's when I first met him. I paid him no attention at first.

He struggled with his thoughts for a while until:

> "He made me want to be smarter."

Because what's the point of being brilliant if nobody gives a shit?

> "He tried."

Hard. Always. He chased the friendship. Showed up. Never gave up.

> "I didn't have to try with my other friends."

They were there because of circumstance — because of shared classes or mutual sarcasm or alcohol.

But Alan? He *worked* for it. He *wanted* Darren as his friend.

And maybe… just maybe… that's what made it so sacred.

Darren stood up and went to the window. Looked out over the campus. Empty this late. Cold.

He remembered the night Alan first asked to sit next to him in IT class. Said it with a grin and that "I know I'm not in your league, but let me be around it anyway" charm.

Darren didn't say yes out of kindness.

He said yes because Alan made him feel like he mattered.

And if he was honest… there wasn't *anyone else* in his life who ever made him feel like that.

Not his housemates.

Not his girlfriend.

Not even his parents, not really.

Alan saw him.

> "You only get one friend like that in life."

He whispered it aloud.

Not for drama.

Just truth.

He sat back down.

And started sketching out the plan.

He would never tell Alan. Not directly. That would risk everything. He needed Alan to *believe* it was still coming for him. Needed the design to *expect* him.

Because Darren had figured something out.

Something deep.

Something horrible.

If death is a law — a fixed appointment — then maybe… *maybe you can switch places in the queue.*

But it has to believe the original is still arriving.

He didn't cry. Didn't flinch.

He just nodded once.

And whispered to himself again:

"He'd do it for me."

And the truth was…
He would have.

Chapter Eighteen – False Calm

Alan had stopped fighting it.

Years had passed — some filled with laughter, others stained with tears.

That's just how life goes.

Into every life, a little rain must fall.
And without the rain, we can never truly appreciate the sun.

The date was set. The time was known.
There was a strange kind of peace in that.

No more tests. No more near misses.
Just time. Precious time. Slipping through the hourglass one quiet day at a time.

He stopped looking for signs.
Stopped checking clocks.
Stopped waiting for the chair to move.

It still did, now and then.
He just chose not to notice.

Instead, he wrote.

Filled pages with thoughts he never expected to put down. Things he wanted to say, not out loud — not even to Darren — but to the version of himself that might live on somewhere, in someone's memory. Maybe Darren's. Maybe nobody's.

They walked a lot in those final days.

Down old paths through Sutton Park.
Through alleyways near their school.
Once even back to the airfield — though neither of them said why.

Darren was quieter than usual, but not in a sad way. Just… content. Watchful. Like someone watching the last act of a play they already knew the ending to.

Alan noticed it once, and asked, "You alright?"

Darren smiled. "Yeah. Just thinking."

"About what?"

Darren shrugged. "Things and stuff."

The night before it happened, they sat in Alan's room. The garden was dark. The koi pond still. Flloyd hadn't surfaced all day — probably sulking in the depths.

Alan poured them both a whisky.

"Reckon I've come to terms with it," he said.

"With what?" Darren asked, not looking up.

"You know."

A pause. Darren let him talk.

"I used to be terrified. But now? I just want it to be quick. I want it to mean something. And I want you to remember I'm okay with it."

Darren stared at his glass.

Alan laughed softly. "You always were the smart one. The brilliant one."

He raised his glass.

"To genius-level friends."

Darren clinked his glass without smiling.

"To one-of-a-kind ones."

They drank.

At midnight, Alan turned in early.

"I want to be rested," he said with a smirk. "Don't want to meet fate with pillow creases on my face."

Darren laughed.

But it didn't reach his eyes.

"Night, Daz."

"Night, Al."

In the other room, Darren opened his laptop one last time.

The line of code was still there.

    A. Carter – 14 May 2043 – 08:17

He deleted it.

It came back.

He didn't try again.

Instead, he closed the lid.

Took a deep breath.

And quietly packed the chair into the boot of his car.

Chapter Nineteen – Eight Seventeen

Alan woke early.

Not from fear — he hadn't felt that in days — but from a strange sense of clarity. The kind you get before a long trip. A knowing. A readiness.

The years had slipped by — quietly, one after another, the way time always does when you're not watching. And yet, looking back, they'd gathered pace somehow… all leading here. To this moment. The one he'd always known would come. Once distant. Now towering above him with a certainty that felt like gravity.

He showered, dressed without rush, poured a tea, and stood by the patio doors watching the garden wake up. The koi were stirring. Even Flloyd surfaced once — breaching the pond like a memory, then sinking again into green.

The house was still. Too still.

He looked at the clock.

07:44

Almost.

He walked to the room.
The room.
The one they'd decided on for "it" to happen.
Not morbid. Just agreed.

It had always felt like the right place — part memory, part mystery, part stage.

Alan opened the door slowly.

The morning light didn't pour in. The curtains were closed. The air was heavy. The room was dark but a light on the ceiling was just barely shedding enough light so that he could see.

And then…
He froze.

Darren was already there.

Sitting.

In the chair.

"Daz?" Alan blinked. "What are you doing?"

Darren didn't answer at first. He looked calm. Centred. As if he belonged there.

"You shouldn't be in the chair," Alan said, stepping forward. "I'm supposed to—"

Then the ceiling light exploded.

A sudden *crack* — like a firework indoors — followed by a rain of shattered glass and a scream of darkness.

Alan reeled back.

Pitch black.

The smell of burnt dust and hot metal. A fizzing wire.
And silence.

"Darren!"

No answer.

Alan's hand slapped at the wall, then stumbled out the door, heart hammering.

He tore down the hallway, flung open the kitchen drawer, grabbed the torch.

08:16

He sprinted back.

Flicked the light on.

The beam cut through dust and shadow.

And found him.

Darren was still in the chair.

Head tilted.

Neck slick with blood.

A jagged shard of glass from the exploded ceiling light — long, razor-clean — was lodged just below his jaw, pulsing gently as his heart tried and failed to keep going.

Alan dropped to his knees.

"No, no, no—"

He pressed his hands over the wound, trying to stop the impossible.

"Darren, stay with me! Come on, mate—come on—"

But Darren wasn't moving.

His eyes fluttered. Locked briefly on Alan.

Tried to say something.

Didn't.

And then…
He was gone.

Alan stayed there a long time.

He didn't scream.

Didn't run.

He just sat, hands soaked, eyes wide.

Whispered things, like:

> "Why would you do that?"

> "You had everything."

> "You were brilliant. Your life was going to be amazing!"

> "I was just a bloody warehouse worker. I wasn't going anywhere."

And then quieter:

> "Why would you do that… for me?"

The torchlight began to dim.

And Alan began to understand.

"He knew."

He spoke it like a confession to the dark.

"He knew the chair was meant for me. And he sat in it anyway."

His voice broke.

"Because… because he knew I would've done it for him."

He reached up. Touched Darren's cold hand.

"And he was right."

The light died.

But Alan stayed there.

Just him.

And the only friend that had ever truly seen him.

Chapter Twenty – Reflection

It's been a year since Darren died.

And I still don't know how to talk about it properly.

Sometimes I forget he's gone. I'll have a thought, or hear something clever, and go to message him. There's a part of me that still expects a reply. That still hears his voice when I walk through certain streets, or sit at the desk where he last stood.

He's *everywhere*.

And nowhere.

People always ask the same thing.

> "Why would he do that for you?"

They don't mean it cruelly — not always — but the words carry weight.

He was the genius.
The millionaire.
The one with potential so sharp it cut every room he entered.

Me?

I was the bloke from the warehouse.
The gamer.
The nobody.

So why?

Why trade all of that for *me*?

I've asked myself that question every day.

I asked it while cleaning the blood from the floorboards.
I asked it when I saw his parents at the funeral and couldn't speak.

I asked it at 8:17 every morning for weeks after — just staring at the clock, waiting for the pain to settle.

But eventually, I found the answer.

He did it because he was my friend.

Not a casual friend. Not a pub mate. Not someone I'd lose touch with after a job change or a woman or a falling-out.

He was *my best friend*.

The kind you only get once in a lifetime — if you're lucky.

And he knew me better than I knew myself.

Darren was brilliant, yeah.

But he wasn't untouchable.
He wasn't cold.
He *felt* things. Deeper than most.

And what he felt, somehow, was that I mattered.

Even when I didn't see it.

He remembered every time I'd showed up. Every dumb joke. Every late-night game. Every moment I'd been the annoying, persistent, loyal little shit who just *wouldn't let him be alone*.

I chased him.

Because I knew.

From the first moment I met him, I knew I'd never meet anyone else like him.

And maybe… just maybe… he came to feel the same about me.

He gave up everything.

Not for fame.

Not for some grand legacy.

He did it for *friendship*.

Because in the end — despite all the logic, all the intelligence, all the reasons not to — he looked at me and decided I was worth saving.

Not because of who I was.

But because I was *his*.

I visit him sometimes.

Sit by the tree where we used to meet as kids.
Bring a fold-out chair. Set it up. Don't sit in it. Just… let it be there.

Let it face the wrong way.

Sometimes, when the wind moves just right, I imagine him there. Legs crossed. Smirking. Saying something sarcastic about my clothes or my tea choice or my thinning hair.

And sometimes, I say it out loud:

> "I'd have done it for you, too."

You don't get many friends like Darren in this life.

And for me…

He was the one.